OUR SOLAR
SYSTEM

Giles Sparrow

Published in 2018 by Enslow Publishing, LLC.
101 W. 23rd Street, Suite 240, New York, NY 10011

Library of Congress Cataloging-in-Publication Data

Names: Sparrow, Giles, 1970- author.
Title: Our solar system / Giles Sparrow.
Description: New York, NY : Enslow Publishing, 2018. | Series: Space explorers | Audience: K to grade 3. | Includes bibliographical references and index.
Identifiers: LCCN 2017016825| ISBN 9780766092679 (library bound) | ISBN 9780766094062 (pbk.) | ISBN 9780766094079 (6 pack)
Subjects: LCSH: Solar system—Juvenile literature.
Classification: LCC QB501.3 .S665 2018 | DDC 523.2—dc23
LC record available at https://lccn.loc.gov/2017016825

Printed in the United States of America

To Our Readers: We have done our best to make sure all websites in this book were active and appropriate when we went to press. However, the author and the publisher have no control over and assume no liability for the material available on those websites or on any websites they may link to. Any comments or suggestions can be sent by e-mail to customerservice@enslow.com.

Picture Credits:
Key: b–bottom, t–top, c–center, l–left, r–right NASA: 7cl (Goddard Space Flight Center/CI Lab), 10bl & 26cr (JPL), 10r, 14cr & 26br, 15br (Goddard Space Flight Center/DLR/ASU), 16tr, 16cr & 27tl, 17tl (JPL-Caltech/ASU), 18cl (JPL-Caltech/UCLA/MPS/DLR/IDA/Justin Cowart), 19tr & 27tr (JPL/MPS/DLR/IDA/Björn Jónsson), 20cl, 22cl, 23tr & 27br, 24br (William Crochot), 28tl, 29tl, 29bl; Shutterstock: cover & title page main (NikoNomad), tl (Vadim Sadovski), bl & 30b (Triff), c (Aphelleon), tr (Vadim Sadovski), br & 31tr (Catmando), 4–5 (Stefano Garau), 4cl (MaraQu), 4b (Viktar Malyshchyts), 4cr (NASA), 5t & 31b (tose), 5br (pixbox77), 6–7 (Vadim Sadovski), 6l & 32 (Mopic), 7t & 26tr (dalmingo), 8–9 (Amanda Carden), 8bl & 26tl (Jurik Peter), 8r (koya979), 9t (21), 10–11 b/g (nienora), 11 (NASA), 11b (21), 12–13 (Anton Balazh), 12l & 26bl (Vlad61), 13t (21), 13b (AuntSpray), 14–15 b/g (Aphelleon), 14–15 (Quaoar), 14br (tovovan), 16–17 (Vadim Sadovski/NASA), 16b (21), 18–19 (Andrea Danti), 18b (21), 20–21 & 20cr & 27cl (Vadim Sadovski/NASA), 20–21 b/g (Yuriy Kulik), 20br (Tristan3D), 21tr (21), 22–23 (manjik/NASA), 22–23 b/g (Triff/NASA), 22b (21), 23c & br (NASA), 24–25 & 27bl (Vadim Sadovski/NASA), 25tr (21), 28b (Vadim Sadovski), 29cr (godrick); Wikimedia Commons: 24cl (Joop van Bilsen/Nationaal Archief NL Fotocollectie Anefo).

Enslow Publishing
101 W. 23rd Street
Suite 240
New York, NY 10011
USA
enslow.com

CONTENTS

Introduction

Our Universe is a huge area of space made up of everything we can see in every direction. It contains a great number of different objects—from tiny specks of cosmic dust to mighty galaxy superclusters. The most interesting of these are planets, stars and nebulae, galaxies, and clusters of galaxies.

Stars

A star is a dense (tightly packed) ball of gas that shines through chemical reactions in its core (middle). Our Sun is a star. Stars range from red dwarfs, much smaller and fainter than the Sun, to supergiants a hundred times larger and a million times brighter.

Planets

A planet is a large ball of rock or gas that orbits (travels around) a star. In our solar system there are eight "major" planets, several dwarf planets, and countless smaller objects. These range from asteroids and comets down to tiny specks of dust.

Nebulae

The space between the stars is filled with mostly unseen clouds of gas and dust called nebulae. Where they collapse (fall in) and grow dense enough to form new stars, they light up from within.

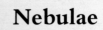

4

Galaxies

A galaxy is a huge cloud of stars, gas, and dust, including nebulae, held together by a force called gravity. There are many different types of galaxy. This is because their shape, the nature of their stars, and the amount of gas and dust within them can vary.

This is our home galaxy, the Milky Way, seen from Earth. Our view of the Universe depends on what we can see using the best technologies that we have.

Galaxy Clusters

Gravity makes galaxies bunch together to form clusters that are millions of light-years wide. These clusters join together at the edges to form even bigger superclusters—the largest structures in the Universe.

The Sun's Family

The solar system is the region of space that surrounds our star, the Sun. It holds billions of objects, from tiny pieces of dust and icy boulders to eight major planets, some of them far larger than Earth.

Eight Planets and More

The planets of the solar system are split into two main groups. Close to the Sun there are four fairly small rocky planets. Earth is the third of these in order from the Sun, and also the largest. Farther out, past a region made up of shards and chunks of rock, there are four much larger worlds: The gas and ice giant planets.

Mars is the outermost of the rocky planets. It is just over half the size of Earth.

Venus, the second planet, is almost the same size as Earth.

The solar system formed from gas and dust left orbiting the newborn Sun about 4.5 billion years ago.

Mercury is the smallest planet and the closest to the Sun.

Earth is the only rocky planet with a large natural satellite, the Moon.

SOLAR SYSTEM PROFILE

Planets: Eight
Radius of orbit of most distant planet, Neptune:
2.8 billion miles (4.5 billion km)
Radius of heliosphere:
11.2 billion miles (18 billion km)
Region ruled by Sun's gravity:
Four light-years across

Where Does It End?

Astronomers haven't agreed on where exactly the solar system comes to an end. Some say it reaches only a little way past the orbits of the planets, just as far as the heliosphere—the region that the solar wind (particles streaming out from the Sun) covers. Others say it reaches as far as the Sun's gravity can hold onto objects: about halfway to the nearest star.

Jupiter is the fifth planet, and by far the largest.

Neptune, the farthest planet from the Sun, is nearly four times bigger than Earth.

Space probes have discovered changes in the solar wind as they leave the heliosphere.

Uranus is an ice giant, quite a bit smaller than Jupiter or Saturn.

Saturn was the most distant planet known in ancient times.

Saturn is famous for its rings. However, all the giant planets have ring systems—they are just a lot fainter.

The Sun

Our Sun is a fairly average, middle-aged star. It doesn't stand out, compared to other stars we know, but the heat, light, and streams of particles it pours out across the solar system set the conditions on Earth and all the other planets.

Solar Features

The Sun's surface is made up of extremely hot gas, with a temperature of around 9,900 °F (5,500 °C). Hot gas from inside the Sun rises to the surface, cools down by releasing light, and then sinks back toward the core. A non-stop stream of particles is also released from the surface, forming a solar wind that blows across the solar system.

Some particles are led toward Earth's poles, creating the aurorae, or northern and southern lights.

Earth's magnetic field shields it from passing solar wind.

The Solar Cycle

Some features on the Sun come and go over time. Dark areas called sunspots form and then disappear, and so do huge loops of gas, called prominences, that rise high above the Sun. Most impressive of all are outbursts called solar flares, which release huge amounts of radiation (energy) and hot gas. All this activity repeats itself every 11 years because of changes in the Sun's magnetic field.

Never look directly at the Sun—it's so bright that you risk damaging your eyes. Astronomers study it with special telescopes.

Prominences are created when gas flows along loops of magnetic field that stick out of the Sun's surface. There is usually a sunspot group at each end.

SUN

Diameter: 864,000 miles (1.39 million km)
Distance: 93 million miles (149.6 million km)
Rotation period: Approx 25 days
Mass: 333,000 x Earth

The surface of the Sun that can be seen is called the photosphere. It marks a region where the Sun's gas becomes transparent.

Dark sunspots are much cooler than their surroundings, with temperatures of about 6,300 °F (3,500 °C).

Mercury and Venus

Two scorching-hot rocky planets orbit closer to the Sun than Earth. Venus is almost the same size to Earth but with a very different atmosphere. Mercury is a tiny world much like our Moon, which speeds around the Sun in just 88 days.

Roasted Surfaces

Temperatures on both Mercury and Venus reach more than 800 °F (430 °C), but Venus is actually hotter than Mercury although it is farther from the Sun. That is because Venus's atmosphere traps heat. This means that the temperature is about 860 °F (460 °C) both day and night. Mercury has no atmosphere, so temperatures on its night side can drop to -280 °F (-170 °C).

Mercury's surface has many craters (holes), like our Moon. This picture has been treated to reveal surface features.

3D view of a Venusian volcano called Maat Mons.

Visiting Venus

Venus's atmosphere is 100 times thicker than Earth's, and is mostly made up of toxic carbon dioxide with sulphuric acid rain. Any human trying to land there would be choked, crushed, and cooked at the same time. Even heavily shielded robot space probes have only lasted for a few minutes. Astronomers have mapped Venus's landscape without landing there, using radar beams that pass through the clouds and bounce back from the surface to show its features.

Venus has a thick, toxic atmosphere that isn't shown in this picture, so that we can see the surface beneath.

This view of Venus uses radar maps from the *Magellan* space probe.

Venus's landscape features volcanoes and cooled, solid lava.

VENUS PROFILE

VENUS

Diameter: 0.5 Earths (12,104 km)
Length of day: 243 Earth days
Length of year: 225 Earth days
Number of moons: None

Our Planet

Earth is the largest of the solar system's rocky planets, and it is also the one with the most interesting surface. Not only is our home world mostly covered in water, but its surface is always changing through a process called plate tectonics.

Earth's atmosphere acts as a blanket. It protects the planet from extreme temperature changes.

World of Water

Earth's orbit around the Sun puts it in a region astronomers call the Goldilocks zone. The temperature across most of the surface is not too hot, not too cold, but "just right" for liquid water. A "water cycle" moves this life-giving chemical between liquid, gas, and solid ice, and helps shape Earth's surface.

The huge amounts of water on Earth help to explain its abundant life. Water is very important for life, because it allows chemicals and nutrients to move around.

12

EARTH

Diameter: 7,918 miles (12,742 km)
Length of day: 23 h 56 m
Length of year: 365.25 days
Number of moons: One

During the water cycle, water vaporizes (becomes a gas) and rises to make clouds in our atmosphere.

Jigsaw Planet

Earth is made up of layers. At its core is solid ball of iron and nickel, with an inner temperature of 9,752 °F (5,400 °C). Above this lies the mantle, made of molten rock, called magma. Earth's thin outer layer, or crust, is a jigsaw puzzle of giant pieces called plates that float on top of the magma. Over millions of years plates move apart or together, changing the shape and size of the continents and oceans.

crust

mantle

Plates move by a few cm (in) each year.

inner core

outer core

The Moon

Highland areas contain countless ancient craters.

Earth's constant partner, the Moon, is the largest natural satellite compared to its planet in our solar system. It is an airless ball of rock covered in craters (bowl-shaped holes) formed when smaller objects smashed into it billions of years ago.

Seas and Highlands

The Moon's surface is a mix of dark, fairly smooth areas called seas or *maria*, and bright, cratered areas called highlands. The seas are what is left over of huge craters that formed about four billion years ago. They were later flooded and then smoothed out by lava erupting from beneath the surface.

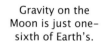

Gravity on the Moon is just one-sixth of Earth's.

Lessons from *Apollo*

Twelve NASA astronauts walked on the surface of the Moon between 1969 and 1972. By studying its rocks and collecting samples they helped us understand the history of the entire solar system—how the planets formed from countless smaller particles crashing together about 4.5 billion years ago. The Moon itself was created when a Mars-sized planet slammed into Earth toward the end of this stage.

MOON PROFILE

Diameter: 2,159 miles (3,474 km)
Distance from Earth: 238,700 miles (384,400 km)
Rotation period: 27.32 Earth days
Length of orbit: 27.32 Earth days

THE MOON

More recent craters spray debris (shards of rock) across the landscape.

Dark seas fill the outlines of large ancient craters.

The first manned Moon landing touched down in the Sea of Tranquility in July 1969.

This radar map shows high areas in yellow and red, and low areas in blue. It clearly shows a huge crater at the Moon's south pole.

Mars

The outermost rocky planet is also the one most like Earth. Mars today is a cold desert with thin, toxic air, but newest discoveries have shown that it used to be much more welcoming, and that it might be again in the future.

Desert Planet?

Mars owes its famous red sands to large amounts of iron oxide, better known as rust. But sand dunes are only one part of the varied Martian landscape. Mars is also home to the largest volcano in the solar system (Olympus Mons, which is currently not active), and the deepest canyon, a huge crack in the surface called the Mariner Valley.

Martian Explorers

Mars is the best explored of all the other planets in the solar system. Many countries have sent space probes to map it from orbit, while NASA has landed wheeled rovers on the surface. Together, the different space agencies have shown that large amounts of water used to flow on Mars (it is now locked away as ice in the upper layers of soil). Is it possible there used to be life on this planet?

Rocks reveal traces of past water.

NASA's *Curiosity* rover has covered more than 9 miles (15 km) of the Martian surface.

MARS PROFILE

Diameter: 4,217 miles (6,789 km)
Length of day: 24 h 37 m
Length of year: 1.88 Earth years
Number of moons: Two

MARS

Two small, lumpy moons called Phobos (left) and Deimos orbit Mars. Astronomers are not sure if they formed alongside Mars, or used to be asteroids.

Bright ice caps at Mars's north and south poles are larger in winter and smaller in summer.

The northern half of the planet is mostly made up of smooth plains.

Air pressure on Mars is less than one percent of Earth's, and the atmosphere is mostly carbon dioxide.

The Asteroid Belt

Between the orbits of Mars and Jupiter lies a wide region of space where most of the solar system's asteroids orbit. Astronomers think there could be a few hundred millon of these rocky and icy worlds, but they are so spread out that it is easy to pass through the belt.

Where Asteroids Come From

The belt is a region where Jupiter's strong gravity stops small objects grouping together to form bigger ones, so no planet could ever form here. When asteroids do crash into each other, they break into smaller objects. The orbits of these objects spread out to form asteroid "families."

This artist's impression (picture) shows the asteroids much more tightly packed than they are in reality.

Ceres's smooth landscape suggests an icy crust.

Ceres

The largest object in the belt, Ceres, is only one third the diameter of Earth's Moon. It is made from a mix of rock and ice that helps to smooth out its landscape. Experts think there could be a layer of salty water hidden beneath the solid crust. The bright patches in the middle of craters may be caused by this water rising to the surface.

DWARF PLANET PROFILE

Name: Ceres
Diameter: 587 miles (945 km)
Length of day: 0.38 Earth days
Length of year: 4.6 Earth years
Mass: 0.00015 Earths

ASTEROID BELT

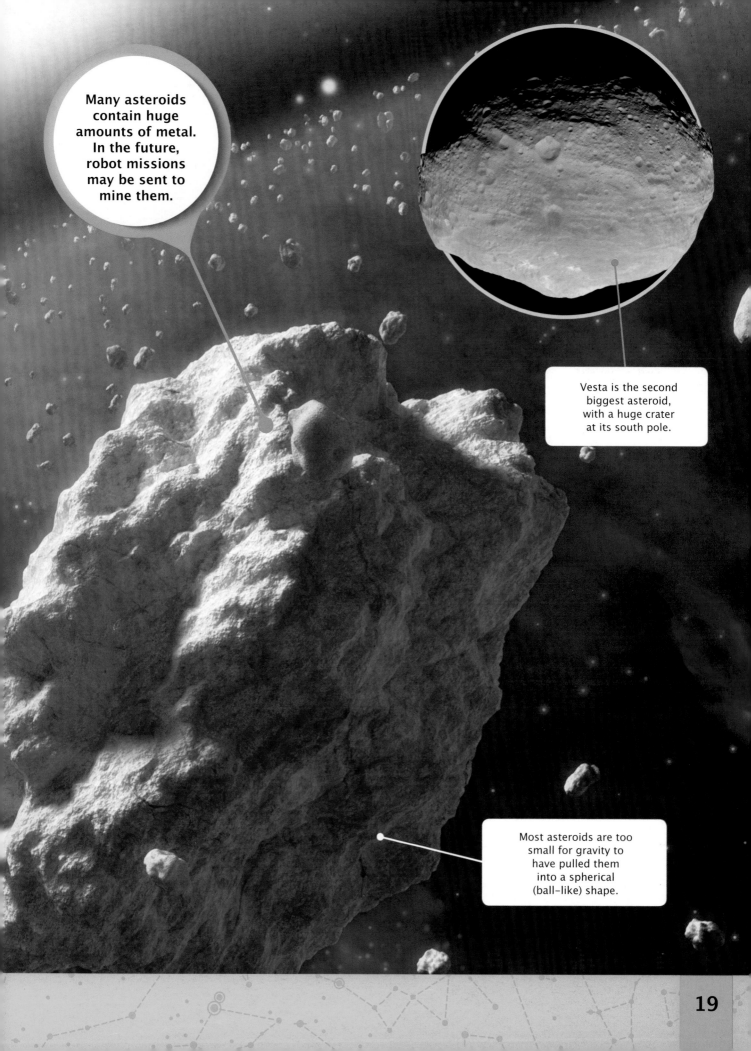

Many asteroids contain huge amounts of metal. In the future, robot missions may be sent to mine them.

Vesta is the second biggest asteroid, with a huge crater at its south pole.

Most asteroids are too small for gravity to have pulled them into a spherical (ball-like) shape.

Jupiter

Named after the ruler of the Roman gods, Jupiter is the largest planet in our solar system. This gas giant is the fifth planet, separated from the four inner, rocky planets by the asteroid belt. Ninety percent of Jupiter's atmosphere is hydrogen gas. Most of the rest is helium.

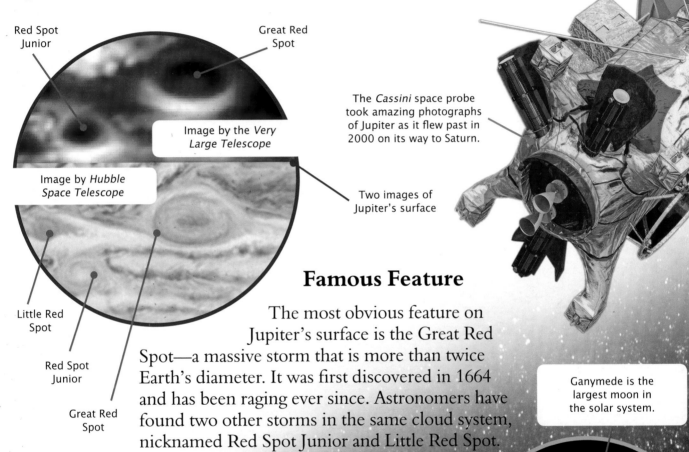

Red Spot Junior

Great Red Spot

The *Cassini* space probe took amazing photographs of Jupiter as it flew past in 2000 on its way to Saturn.

Image by the *Very Large Telescope*

Image by *Hubble Space Telescope*

Two images of Jupiter's surface

Little Red Spot

Red Spot Junior

Great Red Spot

Ganymede is the largest moon in the solar system.

Famous Feature

The most obvious feature on Jupiter's surface is the Great Red Spot—a massive storm that is more than twice Earth's diameter. It was first discovered in 1664 and has been raging ever since. Astronomers have found two other storms in the same cloud system, nicknamed Red Spot Junior and Little Red Spot.

Moons and Rings

Jupiter has more moons than any other planet in the solar system. The four largest—Io, Europa, Ganymede, and Callisto—can be seen from Earth. They are called the Galilean moons, because the Italian astronomer Galilei was one of the first to describe them. Jupiter is also orbited by thin, dark rings of dust.

PLANET PROFILE

Diameter: 88,800 miles (143,000 km)
Length of day: 9h 56m
Length of year: 11.86 Earth years
Number of moons: 67

White bands of cloud are called zones.

Red–brown bands are called belts.

Saturn, Uranus, and Neptune

The three giant planets of the outer solar system are all smaller than Jupiter. Saturn is quite similar to Jupiter, but Uranus and Neptune are "ice giants"—beneath their blue-green atmospheres they are mostly a mix of slushy chemicals including water.

Rings

All four giant planets are surrounded by ring systems, but Saturn's are by far the most impressive. They are made up of trillions of icy particles in orbit above the planet's equator. They often crash into each other, which keeps them in orbit.

This is Titan, the largest of Saturn's 62 moons.

Saturn's rings are thousands of miles across, but are very thin.

SATURN PROFILE

SATURN

Diameter: 72,400 miles (116,500 km)
Length of day: 10 h 33 m
Length of year: 29.46 Earth years
Number of moons: 62

Uranus has 13 rings and 27 known moons.

World on its Side

Most of the solar system's planets are a little tilted in their orbits around the Sun, but only Uranus is completely knocked over on one side. This makes it look like the planet "rolls" along its orbit. It gives Uranus extreme seasons—at the poles, winter is one long night lasting almost 40 years, followed by a summer of about the same length.

Uranus

Saturn's weather bands are like Jupiter's, but the planet's clouds are surrounded by a creamy haze (fog).

Neptune

Storms on Neptune look like dark spots. High clouds seem white.

Pluto and Beyond

Beyond the orbit of Neptune lies a ring of small frozen worlds called "ice dwarfs." Pluto, the most famous of these, was once called a planet in its own right. Even further out is the Oort Cloud, a cloud of icy comets at the edge of the solar system.

The temperature at the surface of Pluto ranges from –360 °F (–218 °C), when it is closest to the Sun, to –400 °F (–240 °C).

Mysterious World

Pluto is a mix of rock and ice about half the size of the planet Mercury. Such a small, distant world should be a deep-frozen ball of ice, but when NASA's *New Horizons* probe flew past in 2015, it showed a surprising world that may have been shaped by volcano-like eruptions of ice a long time ago.

Jan Oort discovered the the cloud that was later named after him by looking at the shapes and directions of comet orbits.

Kuiper Belt

Pluto's orbit

Typical KBO Orbit

Oort Cloud

Kuiper and Oort

The area where ice dwarfs orbit beyond Neptune is called the Kuiper Belt after astronomer Gerard Kuiper. He was one of the first people who thought there was such an area in our solar system. Objects that orbit here are often known as Kuiper Belt Objects (KBOs). From the edge of the Kuiper Belt, the huge Oort Cloud stretches out for almost a light-year, beginning as a broad disk, then opening out into a huge ball of icy, sleeping comets.

DWARF PLANET PROFILE

Diameter: 1,475 miles (2,374 km)
Length of day: 6.39 Earth days
Length of year: 248 Earth years
Number of moons: 5

Pluto's surface is mostly nitrogen, methane, and carbon monoxide ices.

Pluto's biggest moon, Charon, is more than half the size of Pluto itself.

Pluto might have active ice volcanoes even today.

25

Did You Know?

There's always more to learn about what lies in the vastness of space. Boost your knowledge with these amazing facts about our solar system.

Astronomers measure solar system distances in **Astronomical Units** (AU). One AU is 93 million miles (149.6 million km)—the same as the usual distance between the Earth and the Sun.

Because the Sun is not a solid body, different parts of it rotate (spin around) at different rates—its **equator** spins faster than the polar regions.

Venus is the only planet whose day is longer than its **year.**

Water covers **71%** of Earth's surface.

The *Apollo* astronauts brought 840 lb (381 kg) of **Moon rocks** back to Earth.

The Martian moon **Phobos** is falling in a spiral toward the planet. It will smash into it about 50 million years from now.

Jupiter's gravity **kicks** asteroids out of some parts of the asteroid belt, sometimes into orbits that come closer to Earth.

Jupiter is two-and-a-half times **bigger** than the other solar system planets put together.

Some astronomers think that Uranus and Neptune might have **swapped** orbits early in the solar system's history.

Pluto is the god of the **underworld** in Greek myths, but the name is also a nod to Percival Lowell (PL), who built the observatory where it was discovered.

Your Questions Answered

Scientists now know an incredible amount about our solar system, but space is still bursting with amazing information. There are always more questions to be answered and this is what makes people want to become scientists and astronauts. Here are the answers to some interesting questions about space, then you can start asking more!

Where does the dust in space come from?

The dust in space is constantly being recycled as stars and planets go through their life cycles. Dust helps stars to form, and then is either blown away from the star by wind currents that move through space, or is expelled in one go by a star explosion. The dust drifts through space again until it is swept up to become another star.

What are the planets made from?

Mercury, Venus, Earth, and Mars are known as 'rocky' planets. The other planets, Jupiter, Saturn, Neptune, and Uranus are made of gas. Dwarf planet Pluto is also made from rock. The rock of rocky planets consists of metals and minerals. These planets have a hard surface with features such as valleys, volcanoes, and craters.

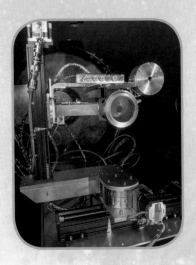

How close can spaceships get to the Sun?

It depends what it is made from, and how quickly or slowly you fly past the sun. Helios 2 is a deep-space probe that has flown to 32 million miles from the Sun's core. In comparison, we are 93 million miles from the Sun. NASA is working on a Solar Probe Plus that is set to launch in 2018. It will fly within 4 million miles of the Sun's surface, withstanding heat of over 2552 °F (1400 °C).

What if an object crashed into the moon today?

The Moon is covered with craters from objects that have crashed into it. With each collision, there is some debris created on impact. If an object was sufficiently large, it could head toward Earth. However, any object drawn toward Earth would burn up in our atmosphere and never reach the surface. It would have to be a very large object to cause any damage to the Moon or Earth.

Who names planets and stars?

The closest five planets in our solar system (Mercury, Venus, Mars, Saturn, Jupiter) were named by the ancient Romans, who named them after their gods. As more planets have been discovered, they have been named in the same tradition. Today, an organization called the International Astronomical Union (IAU) controls naming of all objects or features that are discovered by astronomers.

How long would it take to get to Pluto?

NASA launched its *New Horizons* spacecraft in 2006 and completed its Pluto fly-by in 2015—taking nearly nine and a half years to reach within 8,000 miles. However, this is an incredibly fast spacecraft, the average speed was nearly a million miles a day!

Glossary

asteroid A small rocky object made up of material left over from the birth of the solar system.

astronomical unit Earth's distance from the Sun—about 93 million miles (150 million km).

atmosphere A shell of gases kept around a planet, star, or other object by its gravity.

comet A chunk of rock and ice from the edge of the solar system. Close to the Sun, its melting ices form a coma and a tail.

galaxy A large system of stars, gas, and dust with anything from millions to trillions of stars.

giant planet A planet much larger than Earth, made up of gas, liquid, and slushy frozen chemicals.

gravity A natural force created around objects with mass, which draws other objects toward them.

kuiper belt A ring of small icy worlds directly beyond the orbit of Neptune. Pluto is the largest known Kuiper Belt Object.

light-year The distance covered by light in a year—about 5.9 trillion miles (9.5 million km).

Milky Way Our home galaxy, a spiral with a bar across its core. Our solar system is about 28,000 light-years from the monster black hole at its heart.

Moon Earth's closest companion in space, a ball of rock that orbits Earth every 27.3 days. Most other planets in the solar system have moons of their own.

nebula A cloud of gas or dust floating in space. Nebulae are the raw material used to make stars.

neutron star The core of a supermassive star, left behind by a supernova explosion and collapsed to the size of a city. Many neutron stars are also pulsars.

oort cloud A spherical (ball-shaped) shell of sleeping comets, surrounding all of the solar system out to a distance of about two light-years.

orbit A fixed path taken by one object in space around another because of the effect of gravity.

planet A world that orbits the Sun, which has enough mass and gravity to pull itself into a ball-like shape, and clear space around it of other large objects.

red dwarf A small, faint star with a cool red surface and less than half the mass of the Sun.

rocky planet An Earth-sized or smaller planet, made up mostly of rocks and minerals, sometimes with a thin outer layer of gas and water.

satellite Any object orbiting a planet. Moons are natural satellites made of rock and ice. Artificial (manmade) satellites are machines in orbit around Earth.

space probe A robot vehicle that explores the solar system and sends back signals to Earth.

telescope A device that collects light or other radiations from space and uses them to create a bright, clear image. Telescopes can use either a lens or a mirror to collect light.

Further Information

BOOKS

Daynes, Katie. *See Inside Space.* London, UK: Usborne Publishing, 2008.

DK Reference. *Space!* New York, NY: DK Publishing, 2015.

Green, Jen. *The Sun and Our Solar System* (Great Scientific Theories). Oxford, UK: Raintree, 2017.

Murphy, Glenn. *Space: The Whole Whizz-Bang Story* (Science Sorted). New York, NY: Macmillan Children's Books, 2013.

Newman, Ben. *Professor Astro Cat's Frontiers of Space.* London, UK: Flying Eye Books, 2013.

Rogers, Simon. *Information Graphics: Space.* Somerville, MA: Big Picture Press, 2015.

WEBSITES

www.nasa.gov/kidsclub/index.html
Join Nebula at NASA Kids' Club to play games and learn about space.

www.ngkids.co.uk/science-and-nature/ten-facts-about-space
Get started with these ten great facts about space, then explore the rest of the National Geographic Kids site for more fun.

www.esa.int/esaKIDSen/
Explore this site from the European Space Agency. There's information, games, and news.

Index